Early Prevention Seri

THE LION WHO LOST HIS ROAR

A Story About Facing Your Fears

by Marcia Shoshana Nass
illustrated by Denise Gilgannon

THE LION WHO LOST HIS ROAR

A Story About Facing Your Fears

by Marcia Shoshana Nass
illustrated by Denise Gilgannon

Childswork/Childsplay publishes products for mental health professionals, teachers and parents who wish to help children with their developmental, social and emotional growth.
For questions and comments, call 1-800-962-1141.

A Guidance Channel Company
135 Dupont Street
Plainview, NY 11803

Printed in the United States of America

ISBN 1-58815-004-6

Introduction

Although the vast majority of childhood fears will go away with support and reassurance from parents, some children are more at risk than others of experiencing serious, even debilitating, fears. Some fearful children will develop anxiety disorders, which will make it difficult for them to go to school and/or make friends. Others will be afraid of flying, or crossing bridges, or riding elevators. Still others may be so shy their overall personality development will be affected and, as adults, their lives will be unnecessarily restricted.

But the good news is that fearful children can be helped early in life and, in many cases, even children born with a fearful temperament can become as outgoing and adventuresome as their peers.

In this story Louie the Lion confronts one of the most common human fears, performing in front of others. He learns everyone has some sort of fear and the people who are "brave" have simply learned effective ways of handling their fears and anxieties.

Louie learns he can calm his body down through deep breathing and self-talk. He also learns he must face his fear one small step at a time, a process psychologists call "systematic desensitization."

Of course, one storybook cannot make a fearful child suddenly be able to cope with his/her fears. But, with real-life practice and adult guidance, the psychological techniques introduced in this book can have a meaningful impact on a young child's personality development. However, when a child's fears and anxieties have already progressed to the point where they affect his/her daily life, help from a professional counselor or therapist is recommended.

Lawrence E. Shapiro, Ph. D.
June 2000

Louie the Lion, The Fearless King of the Jungle, lived deep inside a tropical rain forest.

Louie wasn't afraid of pythons or flying lizards. He wasn't even afraid of crocodiles with great big teeth.

Louie wasn't afraid of anything, or so he thought.

Each morning, Louie woke up the jungle with his loud, resounding ROAR-RRRR.

"Wake up to another magnificent day!" bellowed Louie.

From a huge banana tree, Mattie the Monkey spotted King Louie.

Mattie screeched, "Wake up, all you sleepyheads. Hurry, King Louie is coming."

The jungle came alive as animals of all shapes and sizes came from behind the trees and under the rocks and up from the stream.

"How's everyone this morning?" King Louie asked.

"I didn't sleep well at all," said Zachary the Zebra. "I was so-ooooo scared."

"Scared? Of what?" King Louie asked.

"Monsters," answered Zachary.

"Monsters?" laughed King Louie. "Why, that's ridiculous."

"I was scared, too," said Wally the Warthog. "Zachary, Elle and I saw The Night of the Creepiest Monsters at the Jungle-rama Movie Theatre last night, and I bit off all my toenails."

"AWHH," Elle the Elephant boomed. "Don't remind me. Those monsters had ten green eyes, glowing in the dark, oozing gook all over their ugly faces."

Just the thought of the oozing, gooky monsters was enough to make all the animals start screaming.

"E E E K K K K K" echoed through the jungle, rattling tree limbs and stirring the stream.

"Everyone, please calm down," King Louie said.

"Haven't you ever been scared, King Louie?" asked Bobby, a baby tiger.

"Me?" responded King Louie. "Of course not. I am Louie, The Fearless King of the Jungle."

"Not even scared of the dark?" asked Molly the Macaw.

"How about strange sounds?" asked Oliver the Orangutan.

"What about getting lost?" asked Gerald the Giraffe.

"Or of being alone?" asked Terry the Tiger.

King Louie just shook his head "no" to every question. Then he let out a loud ROAR-RRRR.

"I'm not afraid of anything. Now stop being such scaredy cats! And let's get on with the day," said King Louie.

"What's on the calendar for today, Mattie?" asked King Louie.

"We need to make plans for Jungle Jubilee Day. It's only a week away," Mattie said.

"We were thinking of having a party, King Louie," said Elle.

"And we'd like to invite animals from all over the rain forest," said Gerald. "The hummingbirds could deliver the invitations."

"Great idea!" said King Louie.

TODAY'S
CALENDAR
PLAN
JUNGLE
BILEE
DAY!

"There's just one little thing," said Mattie. "We need entertainment."

"I've heard you playing the piano and singing in your lion's den, King Louie. You're really good! Why don't you be the entertainment?" asked Larry the Lemur.

"Oh, I don't know . . ." said King Louie.

"Oh, please, King Louie," the animals begged in unison.

"Well, since you insist, okay," agreed King Louie.

JUBILEE
DAY

The next day, Louie once again let out his loud ROAR-RRRR and awakened all the animals. Then he asked Mattie what was on the calendar for the day.

"A practice rehearsal, King Louie," said Mattie. "The stage is all set up, and Wally and Zachary are moving your piano on to it right now."

"Stage?" King Louie questioned, as he looked toward a large wooden stage with ten steps leading up to it.

"Yes, King Louie, we built a special stage yesterday afternoon just for your performance," explained Mattie.

Louie felt his heart racing.

Ba BOom Ba BOom Ba BOom

As Louie climbed the ten steps up to the stage, his legs felt wobbly. His skin oozed sweat. His cheeks burned.

From high up on the stage, Louie looked down and noticed several of his royal subjects sitting in the audience.

"I didn't know I was going to have an audience for my practice," shouted King Louie.

"The audience will be much, much larger at the party," Mattie shouted back. "Get used to it."

Louie sat down at the piano. Large sweat beads were pouring off him, from everywhere. He had never felt like this before.

"It looks like King Louie is raining," said Molly.

"What's wrong with him?" asked Oliver.

Louie began banging on the piano keys and a horrible noise rattled the jungle. Louie could hardly remember the words to his song.

At the point in the song where he was supposed to let out a loud, boisterous roar, Louie felt a terrible dryness in his mouth. Instead of a great big ROAR-RRRR, all that came out was a little, tiny . . . roar.

ROAR...

The animals giggled so hard the ground shook.

Louie looked out at the audience and thought, "I'm the laughing stock of the entire jungle!"

Louie leaped from the stage and ran all the way home.

25

The next morning, Louie opened his eyes to a new day. It was time to awaken the animals with his great big roar.

"What if I can't roar?" Louie worried. "After last night maybe I won't be able to roar anymore. Oh, my goodness, what if that happens?"

Louie started trembling and sweating at the very thought of the previous morning. He felt his paws become clammy, and his heart started pounding.

Ba BOom Ba BOom Ba BOom

Louie opened his mouth to roar, but not much more than a mouthful of air came out.

"I've lost my roar," Louie thought. "Soon I'll be known as Louie the Scaredy Cat."

BA BOOM

Hours later, Mattie awakened in the banana tree. She could tell from the shadow made by the large rosewood trees that it was almost noon.

"Why didn't King Louie roar us awake?" Mattie worried, as she quickly swung over to King Louie's.

"King Louie, are you all right?" she asked.

"Just call me 'Louie' from now on," he answered. "I'm not The Fearless King of the Jungle anymore. I'm just Louie the Scaredy Cat."

"Oh, King Louie, don't talk like that," begged Mattie.

"This morning, I couldn't even roar my jungle wake-up call," said King Louie.

"You just have a case of stage fright. Yesterday's rehearsal really shook you up. Don't worry. We'll figure out what to do," Mattie promised.

Later that afternoon Louie watched as Wally and Zachary put the piano back in the center of his lion's den.

"Now here's the plan, King Louie," said Wally. "When we leave, we want you to sit at your piano, all alone, and see if you can play and sing and roar, all by yourself."

"Just say to yourself 'Relax. Be calm. Be peaceful.' Then take some deep breaths," said Mattie.

"You've got to tell yourself you can do it," said Zachary.

"But what if I can't?" asked King Louie.

"You've got to stop thinking you can't and start thinking you can," advised Mattie.

After his three friends left, Louie stared at the piano for a long time. Then he closed his eyes and took several deep breaths. "Relax. Be calm. Be peaceful," he told himself, over and over.

Louie played the piano okay. He sang okay. But when it came time to roar, he had trouble.

"Oh, what's the use? That little, tiny, embarrassing roar is going to come out again," Louie thought.

Then Louie remembered what Mattie said, and he changed his thinking. "I can do it! Relax. Be calm. Be peaceful."

Louie opened his mouth and a ROAR came out, not a great big one, but not a tiny, little one, either.

..RELAX...
..BE CALM...
..BE PEACFUL...

Mattie came over a few hours later, and King Louie told her the good news.

"That's great," said Mattie. "Now try to perform in front of me."

"Oh, I don't know if I can do that," said King Louie.

"Of course you can. Go ahead," said Mattie. "It's just me."

Louie played the piano, sang the song, and even roared a little.

"Well," smiled King Louie. "I can play in front of an audience of one."

"Let's invite Molly, and you can play for an audience of two," said Mattie. "When you can play in front of the both of us, we'll add Zachary and Elle, and then Gerald, Wally, Larry, Terry, Bobby and Oliver."

Within a few days, Louie's den was filled with animals listening to him play, sing and roar.

Louie was really quite content until Mattie said, "Now for the next step. Let's move the piano onto the stage."

"Stage?" King Louie asked. "Oh, no, not that stage, with all those steps, again. What if I can't?"

And all the animals shouted back. "But you can."

First, Louie played, sang and roared all alone on stage. Then Mattie sat on the piano and watched.

After Louie felt comfortable performing on stage with Mattie watching, Molly sat in the audience section. And then Zachary and Elle joined Molly. Then Gerald, Wally, Larry, Terry, Bobby and Oliver sat down.

One by one, they invited other animals to sit in the audience, too.

"You can do it," said Mattie. "See, I knew you could."

ROAR

Just then, the hummingbirds flew in.

"We reached all the edges of the rain forest," Charlie, the lead hummingbird, announced. "525 animals, 1,000 bugs and 230 tropical birds are coming to Jungle Jubilee Day."

The color drained from Louie's face.

"I can't perform in front of that big a crowd," said King Louie. He began trembling and sweating again. His heart pounded.

Ba Boom Ba Boom Ba Boom

"It's final," said King Louie. "I can't do it!"

"What do you mean? Jungle Jubilee Day is tomorrow," said Mattie.

"Oh, juggle some coconuts for entertainment," said King Louie.

The animals and birds watched King Louie walk away. And, King Louie didn't turn back.

BABOOM

The next day was Jungle Jubilee Day.

As Mattie climbed the stairs to the stage and took the microphone in her hand, she thought, "I guess I will just have to juggle some coconuts."

"Welcome to Jungle Jubilee Day. As it turns out, I must tell you that Louie, The Fearless King of the Jungle, will...."

WELCOME

Just then, Louie walked on stage wearing a tuxedo and his crown of many jewels. The audience applauded. Mattie couldn't believe her eyes.

Smiling, Mattie said, "As it turns out Louie, The Fearless King of the Jungle, will be performing his new song The Lion's Roar."

The spotlight was on Louie.

As Louie took a few deep breaths, he remembered how he felt when he played for his friends.

"Relax. Be calm. Be peaceful," Louie thought, over and over.

RELAX...
BE CALM...
BE PEACEFUL...

Louie looked out into the audience and saw his friends smiling at him. He was ready. He began playing and singing his song.

At the point where Louie needed to roar, he took a few deep breaths and thought to himself, "Relax. Be calm. Be peaceful."

Louie, The Fearless King of the Jungle, opened his mouth and let out a loud, resounding, boisterous,

ROAR-RRRRRRRRRRRRRRRRRRRRRRRRRRR.

The audience's applause vibrated through the jungle.

ROARRR

Later that night, Louie's friends gathered in his lion's den for a sleepover party.

Louie was about to turn out the light when he remembered Molly was afraid of the dark.

"Do you want me to leave the little light on, Molly?"

"No," said Molly. "I've been using a dimmer on my light every night for the past week. Each night I dimmed the light a little more, and now I can sleep in the dark."

"I'm proud of you, Molly."

"I'm proud of you, King Louie."